W9-CFE-676

Piggies

Dedicated to Marjane Wood

For information about permission to reproduce selections from this book,
please write Permissions, Houghton Mifflin Harcourt Publishing Company
215 Park Avenue South NY NY 10003.

www.hmhbooks.com

Voyager Books is a registered trademark of Harcourt, Inc.

Library of Congress Cataloging-in-Publication Data
Wood, Don, 1945–
Piggies/Don and Audrey Wood; illustrated by Don Wood.
p. cm.
"Voyager Books"
Summary: Ten little piggies dance on a young child's
fingers and toes before finally going to sleep.
ISBN 978-0-15-256341-7
ISBN 978-0-15-200217-6 pb
ISBN 978-0-15-202638-7 board
[1. Bedtime — Fiction. 2. Games — Fiction. 3. Pigs — Fiction.]
I. Wood, Audrey. II. Title.
PZ7.W84737P1   1991
[E] — dc20   89-24598

SCP   29 28 27
4500442801

Printed in China

The paintings in this book were done in oil on Bristol board.
The display type was set in Caxton Book.
The text type was set in Goudy Catalogue.
Composition by Thompson Type, San Diego, California
Color separations by Bright Arts, Ltd., Singapore
Printed and bound by RR Donnelley, China
Production supervision by Warren Wallerstein and Michele Green
Designed by Michael Farmer

Piggies

WRITTEN BY

DON AND AUDREY WOOD

ILLUSTRATED BY

DON WOOD

Harcourt, Inc.

Orlando Austin New York San Diego London

I've got two

fat little piggies,

two smart

little piggies,

two   long

little piggies,

two silly

little piggies,

and two wee

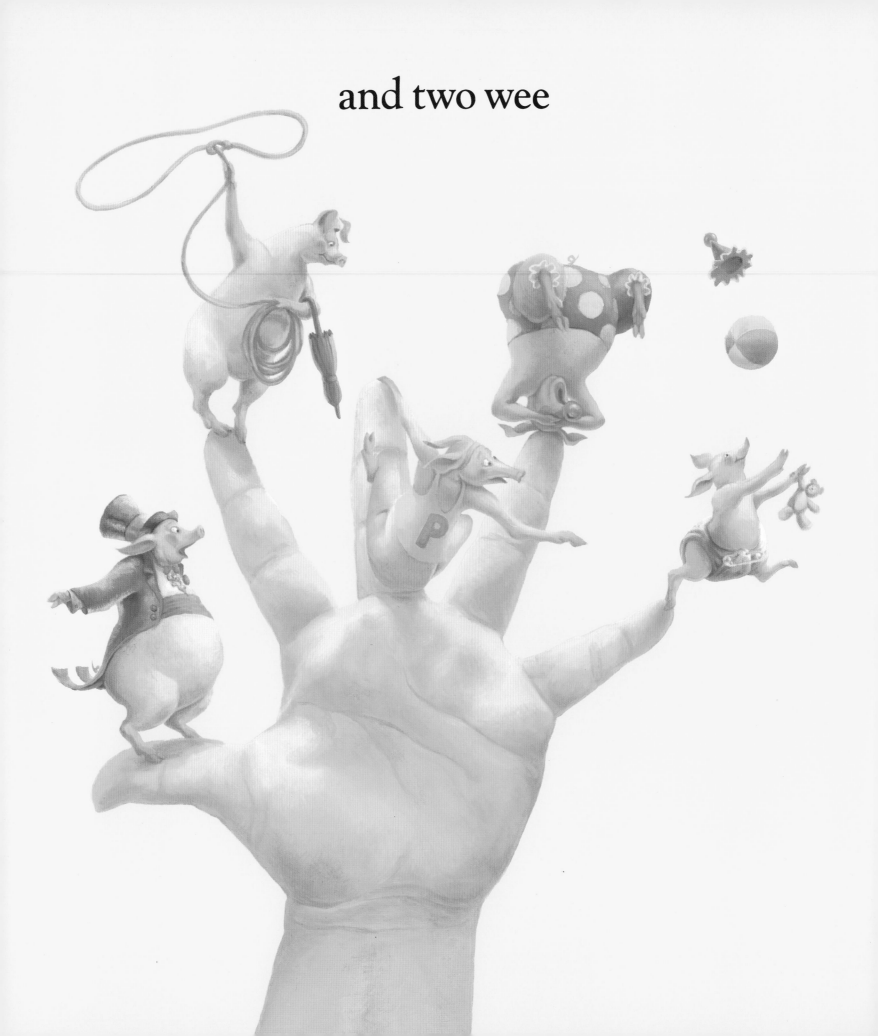

little piggies.

hot little piggies,

and sometimes they're

cold little piggies.

Sometimes they're

clean little piggies,

and sometimes they're

dirty little piggies.

Sometimes they're

good little piggies,

but not at bedtime. That's when

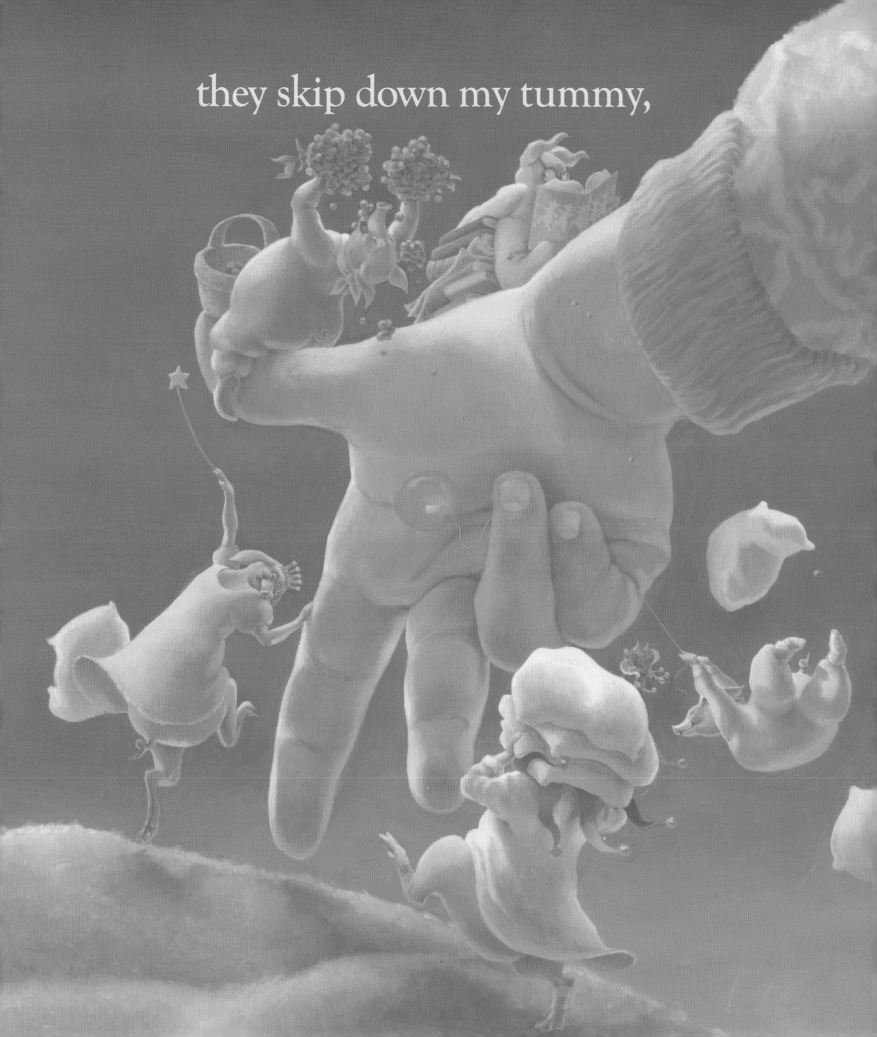

they skip down my tummy,

dance on my toes,

then run away and hide.

So . . .

. . . I put them together, all in a row,
for two fat kisses,
two smart kisses,
two long kisses,
two silly kisses,

and two wee kisses goodnight.

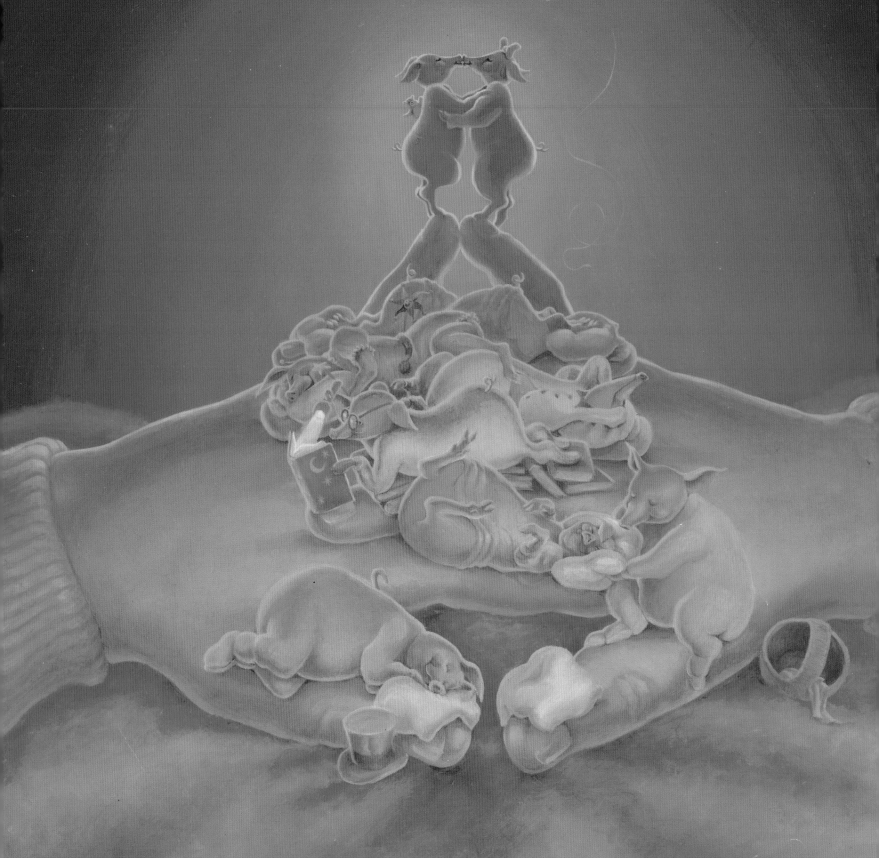